She Grabbed Her
White Jacket

A GUIDE TO THE KEY OF LIFE

Annie Clark

This is a work of fiction created by the author; additional contributions have been provided by book contributors. Any resemblance to actual events or persons outside of the author and/or her contributors is entirely coincidental.

For purchasing information for club, group, educational, or business use, contact:
bravuralifestrategies@gmail.com

Author is available for speaking engagements, book signings/discussions, workshops, and events. Forward inquiries to:
bravuralifestrategies@gmail.com

DEDICATION

I dedicate this book to all the young ones out there
who have yet to claim their brilliance.
May you pave the road that was once less traveled and
may I live to bask in your glory!

CONTENTS

INTRODUCTION

They say necessity is the mother of invention—well, I say, so is survival of an identity crisis—a sudden and complete loss of oneself. And in my case, the self I didn't know I hated.

In 2009 my life crashed. I found myself in a terrifying dark place where I knew I couldn't stay. The most important thing I will tell you is this: I know what it's like to be stuck, broken down, beaten, defeated, helpless, trapped, depressed, tongue-tied, anxious, and worst of all, alone; no one can help, no one understands, and nobody gets it. I drove myself there by my inability to just be myself. I was a life-long victim of seeking to sustain my identity by getting my value from how much I could produce and how perfect I could perform, while desperately seeking approval from others and trying to rescue them from their own pain, as well.

This was a recipe for an exhausting disaster. And the worst part wasn't losing my home, my business or my retirement. It was that I had no self-worth, no me to help myself—just sheer terror. My life imploded. I hit rock bottom and endured years of debilitating panic attacks and PTSD, which resulted in the most profound, prolonged, and painful learning experiences I knew were possible. After this debilitating setback, it was clear that it was me that had beaten me down, me that held me hostage, and only I could heal myself and lead myself. With tremendous support and a drive to survive, I was finally able to claw my way out. During the years of this process, and unbeknownst to me at the time, I developed my own revolutionary, realistic, result-driven method to find and sustain happiness—the HOW!

And so it began...

As I mastered liberation of myself, I set out without knowing what my final route would be. I was willing and prepared to embrace vulnerability and the unknown, and just start somewhere. I healed the broken me and was willing to start over every day with love and be present to meet myself where I was at.

It's been (and continues to be!) quite a ride. Today I'm literally living my dream, while ushering others out through the same exit I used. I continue to lead myself authentically by my truth and others through theirs.

Life's too short not to get what you want, baby!

Author's note: *you may soon be wondering, so here's a tip—Auryn's name is pronounced "our'win"*

ANNIE CLARK

AND SO IT BEGINS...

Tomorrow was the day to make the move, the day to walk away. Lying in bed, the Mother sleepily closed her eyes and asked, "Are you sure we need to leave?"

The Father gently replied, "If Auryn stays here, she'll be altered. It's best we raise her there and stick with the plan."

"I'd be lying if I said I wasn't scared, but I do trust you."

"She can be natural there. She won't know how to be anything other than herself."

"Who will she be?" the Mother asked.

"She will show us."

"What should I be doing then?"

"Be curious, watch, listen, learn."

"I'm sooo nervous…"

"If she falls, we will guide her."

THE JOURNEY

For some, moving could be difficult. Auryn had never known anything other than this home and this place, where people were so warm and their intentions true. This would be a change, an unknown, but one she felt prepared for. Sighing softly, she packed her last box.

Out of her open door, she could spy her Father's desk, where he leaned back in his chair tapping a pen to his mouth in thought. Auryn grinned at the man who had taught her everything. It was inspiring to see him in action.

Her Father was wise, empathetic, a gentle listener. She wanted to be like him more than anything, but he encouraged her to embrace his traits in her own way. Like him, she had dreams to create a grand plan to work toward helping others. She didn't have his experience, but she knew she was as capable as he was.

This move would assist her goal and her grand plan, she thought to herself, and she was more than ready. With her final box taped up, she took it out to the moving van. School would start tomorrow and so would her new life. Once her final box was loaded, she happily skipped back indoors.

THE ARRIVAL

Auryn awoke in her new home filled with optimism. She had a smile on her face that refused to go away as she prepared for the day. Brushing her hair, eating food, getting changed…nothing would make it disappear. When her Father dropped her off at school, she almost forgot to say goodbye. After a quick "Love you!" she tumbled through the door and into her new school.

Her first instinct was to greet the other kids, to reach out. But as she waved, she was met with hesitant responses and weird looks. Auryn felt, for the first time in her life, genuinely unarmed and off guard. She steadied herself and didn't let that get to her. When the bell signaled her first class, she was even bouncier than when she initially walked in. Taking her seat near the front, she watched others file in.

"Welcome back, everyone," the teacher announced, "I'd like to introduce a new student, Auryn. She just moved here."

Auryn skipped her way to the front and waved to the students who she was certain in time would become her new friends.

"I'm excited to meet all of you!" she cheered.

The teacher cleared her throat and got serious, "Now everyone, please be sure to make Auryn feel comfortable and welcome. With that being said, time to share my plans for class today."

Auryn made her way to her seat, but now she was confused. Make her feel welcome and comfortable? She was already comfortable. Why wouldn't she be? That's fine, she told herself, I'll learn in time.

As she watched the other kids, she noticed a group of girls passing notes to one another, snickering and talking. She found it amusing and yet strange that they were just keeping to themselves. She turned her head and saw a girl in the back of the room who was intently watching those girls talk.

When Auryn found the time right, she got up to go ask her, "Do you want to talk to them?"

The girl was startled by Auryn's sudden appearance. She tucked her chin down so her hair fell into her face even more than it had before. "No! I don't."

Auryn was even more confused, silently asking herself: But she was watching them, why didn't she just reach out?

The rest of the day went the same, and Auryn felt herself more and more confused. When she got home, her Father asked, "How was your day, honey?"

"This isn't like home at all..." Auryn sighed, "everyone here is different, they keep to themselves."

This presented her Father's first challenge—to let her find her way, giving her only support, asking questions, listening. "How so?" he thoughtfully asked.

"It's like everyone is looking to figure out what to do or how to be based on what others might think about them. Some kids act out or say bold things, which causes the kids around them to behave differently. I'm not sure, Father, but I think I might be able to help."

Her Father knew he had to curb his instinct to reveal the truth of this world. He was committed to stick with the plan and let Auryn feel new emotions.

She lay in bed that night motivated to understand, and like her Father, be the hero.

The next day at school, Auryn decided she was going to gather as much information and understanding as she could. She thought of her new friend, or soon to be friend—the girl who liked to hide behind her hair. She seemed so shy, yet approachable, and Auryn thought she'd be a good informant. She sought her out and learned her name was Emma. They made plans to talk at lunch.

Auryn entered the lunchroom with hope, Emma had said they'd be eating together, but as she looked around, she didn't see her. Auryn decided to find them a seat and that's when, again, she was caught off guard.

"Is anyone sitting here?" she asked a group of pretty-looking girls. She admired their hair, makeup, and their sense of style. But she was dazed when they all looked at her, looked to each other, snickered, and one said, "Um, these seats are taken."

Auryn didn't debate it. She moved on noticing there were a few more open seats at a table of athletic-looking boys. She admired their sense of humor and closeness. The smiles on their faces seemed almost contagious as she approached. Again she asked, "Is anyone sitting here?" This time she didn't even get a response, which somehow felt like more of a letdown than if she had.

"That's fine, thanks anyway," she said to them. Surely another table could provide her with a couple seats.

Glancing around, she couldn't find any open tables aside from those two. As most of the kids had already cleared the lunch line and squeezed in at other tables, she noticed the seats those girls had said were taken still remained bare. Auryn thought, that's ok, maybe they counted wrong. She doubled back and took those two spots, smiling despite the strange looks from the pretty-looking girls. She knew she had done nothing wrong.

As Auryn ate her lunch, smiling thoughtfully while listening to the other girls, she noticed the shy face of her friend Emma peeking in.

"Emma! Hey! Over here!" Auryn threw both arms up, waving excitedly for her friend to come over.

This made Emma flush, her brown hair falling over her face as she shuffled toward the table. All eyes in the lunchroom made their way to Emma, causing the blush to creep down her neck.

"Next time just wave me over," Emma muttered. She opened her lunchbox and shrank into the table, her eyes refusing to look around even after the staring stopped.

"Why?" Auryn raised an eyebrow.

"I just don't like people looking at me… Did we have to sit here?" Emma hesitantly took a bite of her sandwich.

"What's wrong with right here?" Auryn asked, the small smile never leaving her face.

"Nothing," Emma sighed, "it's nothing."

The car can be a great place for self-reflection and planning. Every time Auryn stared out the window, she didn't see the passing city; instead, she saw her plans for the rest of her school year.

"It seems you have a lot on your mind," her Father mentioned.

"I do. Today was great, but kids here are different. I don't really understand, I can't get to know them, they separate and group up."

Her Father's eyes gazed at her from the rear-view mirror, "Why do you think that is?"

"I don't know."

"What are you feeling?"

"Kinda strange." She rested her head on her hand, watching the clouds, but not really seeing them.

"What do you need?" her Father asked, breaking her reverie.

"Nothing right now, but I'll let you know."

"I have no doubts, I'm here for you if you need me."

"We'll see what tomorrow brings." Self-assured, she knew she would welcome whatever was to unfold.

That night tucked into her bed, Auryn looked at the ceiling thankful for her Father's love, knowing he was always there.

"Tomorrow is a new day," she whispered with enthusiasm.

Her eyes closed as she held onto the knowledge that things will get better—they have to.

"Tomorrow is a new day."

When Auryn arrived at her first class the next day she took a spot next to Emma. She tried to focus, but the words from the teacher came out like gibberish and the words on the board looked like symbols or drawings. How could she focus when there were a million questions buzzing in her mind? She couldn't take it.

"Can you help me understand," she leaned over, gazing at Emma, "why does everyone separate like that?"

"I don't know." Emma barely looked up from her writing.

"Don't you want to be friends with everyone?" Auryn tilted her head, her full attention on Emma.

"I guess, but that's not how it is." Emma waved her

hand dismissively, refusing to glance over.

"If you had to guess, why is that?" Auryn persisted.

Emma sighed before turning to Auryn, "Because, not everybody is the same."

"Do you like it that way?" Auryn asked with curiosity.

"No. It doesn't feel good."

Auryn could feel her opening up a bit, despite her discomfort. "Do the other kids like it that way?"

"I hope not."

A verbal cue from the teacher caused both Auryn and Emma to snap back to focus.

As the bell rang, Auryn felt a burst of excitement knowing she was heading to gym class. She ran around all the time as a kid so she was excited to have the opportunity to let out all her bundled-up energy.

Sitting on the concrete bench, Auryn changed into her gym clothes. A blonde girl, the only other girl in her row of lockers, caught her eye.

"Are you new here?" the stranger asked.

"Yeah, I'm Auryn."

"Beatrice," she scooted closer.

"Please tell me gym is a bit more eventful than normal class?" Auryn smiled hopefully.

"I'd say so, but I do cheerleading, so I'd say I'm biased."

"How cool! Is it fun?"

"It can be, when you've got good friends on the

13

team."

"I'd love to try it," Auryn thought aloud.

"Tryouts are next Tuesday. Why don't you come over to my house and we can practice?"

"That sounds like fun!"

Beatrice's backyard was a great place for cartwheels and tricks. Exhausted, the two rested in the grass, smiling up at the sky.

Auryn turned her head, "Why is everyone so split up here? They're all in groups that don't seem to mix. It doesn't make sense."

Beatrice explained, "Not everybody is nice—there are so many different kinds of people. They just get into these tight cliques and aren't interested in getting to know anyone else or let anyone new in."

This was all news to Auryn. At home, everybody knew everybody pretty well. Sharing, mutual love, and acceptance were a part of daily life. "This is all so new to me. Back at home, no matter how different everyone was, we'd try to get along and appreciate each other. Differences didn't keep us apart."

"You were lucky! I wish it was like that here."

What Beatrice said rang in Auryn's mind, even as she got into the car with her Father. She thought, why couldn't it be like that here?

"Was today any better?" her Father asked, focusing his eyes on the road.

"Totally," was all Auryn could muster. As she

looked out the window, she felt like all the pieces were coming together, all the plans and ideas for bringing her old home here. It made her excited and gave her hope. She wondered if this was how her Father felt when the puzzles in his head were coming together.

MEETING DANIEL

The next day greeted her like an old friend. The optimism and the promise of new ideas led the way while she followed along. She almost danced down the hallway in the morning until the harsh yelling of kids cut through the music in her mind.

"Don't touch me, frickin' queer!" was the first sentence she could make out. Do kids really talk this way, she wondered, peering around the corner.

The target of this statement didn't even speak, he just kept his head down. Auryn didn't even know people could make someone so defenseless they couldn't even speak.

"Gonna say anything? Or are you too much of a coward, faggot?"

Auryn watched as the victim of this verbal assault was pushed down, not even once did he look up. When the kids finally walked away, all he did was bring his knees to his chest.

Walking over to him, Auryn crouched down and put a hand on his shoulder, "Hey, I'm here if you need a friend."

He didn't respond, but the sharp intake of breath

hinting at a sob let her know he heard her.

"What's up with those guys?" she asked.

"I wish I knew...but it's fine, I don't care," he still wouldn't glance her way.

"I'm here to listen," Auryn simply stated, her voice unwavering.

"They always do this. It's not the first time," tears started to roll down his cheek and he tried to wipe them away.

"It's ok, you need to let it out." She rubbed circles into his back with the palm of her hand as he shook a little, starting to sob. "I'm sorry this happened to you. You don't deserve it," she said in his defense.

"Nobody really does things like this for me," he choked out, "I'm not used to it, sorry."

Auryn's shock must have shown on her face because he looked at her like he had said something wrong, his blue eyes tinged with another kind of fear.

"It's fine...it's just...why wouldn't anyone offer help? Are kids here really like that?"

"People don't talk to me, that's all. Maybe it's different for the other kids."

This needs to be different, Auryn thought, someone has to do something.

"Why don't you sit with me and some friends at lunch. We can make sure this doesn't happen to you again." He looked encouraged. "What's your name?" she asked and extended a hand to help him up. He took it.

"Daniel."

They walked down the hallway toward class.

"Oooh, does Daniel have a girlfriend?" a kid teased. Auryn realized he hadn't let go of her hand.

She was about to interject when Daniel gave her hand a squeeze and boldly stated, "No, actually, I'm gay." A palpable burst of confidence soared through his body.

Auryn was impressed by Daniel's confidence as well as the shocked expression on the bully's face. All Daniel needed was some support, a hand to hold, and he could do it by himself.

As the two walked away, Daniel had a smile on his face, "I can't believe it. That's the first time I've really said it out loud."

"I'm proud of you," Auryn said, her cheerful expression saying the same.

Auryn was lost in thought. All it took was letting Daniel know someone out there was with him and he could start to embrace who he truly was. If it worked with Daniel, why not with other kids? She bundled these thoughts up as the bell rang, strolling toward her first class.

As lunchtime began, Auryn found an empty table, allowing for her three new friends to gather. The smiles on their faces were infectious. She saw Emma brighten for the first time, laughing at a joke Daniel told. It was inspiring. They all seemed so different, and yet they were getting along like old friends. If this was possible among a group of three, why not more?

It finally clicked, she needed to follow her Father's example. By encouraging and supporting others to embrace who they are, like he does with her, maybe she could help tear down the restrictive walls that hindered other kids from understanding themselves and one another. The idea had her so excited she could barely form words. She kicked her legs happily under the table, simply relishing in the joy she had brought to three new people. She found herself fantasizing about the future, knowing it would be promising.

Back at home again with her Father, the sun was setting. She was in an armchair, doodling pictures of the patterns she could make out in the wooden table. A face here, a cloud there, all so fascinating.

Her Father set a mug of tea for her onto the table. It brought her back to the land of the living. He didn't ask what she was thinking as he sat down in the chair next to her, all he did was give her an encouraging glance.

"I've got it," she simply stated, tapping her pencil onto the notebook methodically.

"What do you have?" he asked with curiosity, bringing his own mug to his lips.

"I'm gonna gather up a group of people and inspire each of them to be true to who they are!" She was too thrilled to even think about drinking the tea her Father made for her. Instead, she hummed happily to herself, silently appreciating the colors of the setting sun.

"What gave you this idea?"

"I helped a kid who was getting bullied today and even though he was scared, he spoke up to one of them and owned who he was. I want that for everyone." To illustrate the scope she imagined, she extended her arms in a grand gesture, reaching up to the ceiling and far beyond.

While he always supported his daughter, he didn't always understand—he didn't need to. Her desire to help was natural, he raised her empathetically, always listening, always caring. He had faith in who she was—but even so, he had his concerns about her new plan. It was too grand, he thought.

"I'm proud of you. I'm glad you can offer light to kids who are stuck in the dark." He didn't want to deter her from her ideas or make her doubt herself. He knew if she fell, he'd be there to support her. It was all he could do.

"Thank you. I'm nervous, but in that excited nervous way," she giggled, finally taking her first sip.

"Once you're done, let's get ready for bed. Brains need lots of rest to have the clarity to do everything right."

FINDING LENA

Gym again—the moment the teacher announced they'd be running "The Mile" the class let out a collective groan. Auryn looked to Beatrice, who simply shrugged.

"I see it as a way to gain stamina, not like a chore," Beatrice giggled.

"I like that way of thinking about it," as she said it, Auryn couldn't help but giggle too.

Kids began running at their own pace around the track field, they had to run around it four times in order to complete the mile. Auryn tried to keep up with Beatrice, but she could only run so fast and that didn't bother her.

As she slowly jogged, a kid approached from behind and was on pace to pass her. It was the kid who was bullying Daniel the day before. He looked at her, then slowed his pace to match hers.

"You're Daniel's little friend, aren't you?" he asked.

"Yeah, I am," Auryn proudly announced. She'd be friends with anyone, she knew no shame.

"What, are you gay too?" he laughed, giving her arm a shove.

"No, but if I was that's not a bad thing, you know," Auryn said, trying to keep her voice calm and assured.

"Yeah, sure. Only fags hang out with other fags," he tried to run ahead as he said that, but a strong arm hooked him and knocked him to his knees.

He looked shocked as he came up from his fall. Auryn stopped, noticing the girl now standing in front of him.

"You can't just say things like that to people!" the girl yelled. She must have been the one who knocked him over.

"Yeah whatever, Lena," he crossed his arms.

"Why do you think that's okay, making someone feel bad about who they are?" Lena asked.

This girl gets it, Auryn thought, still watching.

"Whatever, you're weird too. Now get out of my way and let me keep running. I have a record to beat."

Lena rolled her eyes and walked to Auryn, but not before plucking a dandelion from the ground.

"Sorry, are you okay?" Lena handed the flower over.

"He doesn't get to me," Auryn put the yellow bloom into her hair.

"That's good. You're Auryn, right?"

Auryn nodded, "Thanks for getting him to go away. I could have done it though."

Lena smiled, "You don't always need to face things on your own."

"That's a good way of thinking. I like you!"

"I try to like me too," Lena sheepishly replied.

What does that mean, Auryn questioned, but shrugged it off as the two started walking.

"Shouldn't we jog like the rest of the kids?" Auryn asked, looking up at Lena.

"I like going my own pace," she said, while gazing up at the blue sky.

Gym was good that day. Auryn left satisfied that she had welcomed another into her group of friends. In time she'd gather everyone, she just had to go at her own pace.

"Hey, it's almost Tuesday!" Beatrice said, sliding onto the bench next to Auryn. It was Friday after dismissal and Auryn was sitting watching buses pass by, taking kids home with them. She wondered what it'd be like to ride one, would it be fun?

When Beatrice didn't get a reply, she continued, "Soooo...I'm thinking I'll invite Daniel, Emma, and Lena to watch us at tryouts. Won't that be fun?"

"My favorite people!" Auryn exclaimed, now paying full attention.

"I knew you'd like that! I want you all to meet my mother, she'll love you guys."

"Stop, I'm getting too excited!" Auryn laughed and grabbed Beatrice's hand, smiling.

"This is my bus. Does it sound like a plan?" Beatrice asked, getting up.

"For sure!" Auryn watched her friend go, wondering how she got so lucky.

While Auryn sat there, her Father parked behind the bus. He was so thankful to see that she was making good friends.

BEATICE'S MOTHER

The weekend passed by with Auryn doing things that made her happy—art, writing, talking with her Father. She knew one day she'd have to write a story about all this, life was too wonderful not to jot down.

Monday was also as normal as it could get except that her friends were happier and more vibrant now that they had found each other. Auryn sat at lunch, listening to Daniel explain the mechanics of his favorite game, knowing she did the right thing helping him feel so confident.

On Tuesday, changing into her gym clothes and running outside to the field, she got her first nerves in anticipation of trying out. She knew that no matter what the outcome, she'd be happy. Daniel, Emma, and Lena watched from the bleachers, which were pretty empty, aside from a few parents. She waved and they waved back.

She and Beatrice had practiced and practiced for

this day. Auryn had bruises from all the handstands, cartwheels, and flips. But it was so worth it when tryouts were complete.

She pumped her fist in the air as she followed Beatrice to where they had set their things. They grabbed their water bottles then went to celebrate with their friends.

"Nice!" Daniel cheered, giving Beatrice a high five. She beamed, taking a drink. As Auryn did the same, she glanced up over her water bottle. An adult woman, with the same blonde hair as Beatrice, was looking at her with confusion. Auryn thought this must have been her mother, but why was she so confused? Her friends were some of the nicest, best people. How could this mother not see that?

Auryn tried to talk too, but her eyes kept darting toward Beatrice's mother. What was she thinking? Auryn had never worried about the thoughts of another person before. She fidgeted with worry. Auryn knew, at the end of the day, this wouldn't get to her. She was strong enough not to let any temporary anxieties get her down.

Finally, Beatrice waved the woman over, "Mom, Mom! Meet my new friends!"

Her mother walked over, "Well, it's nice to meet you all." She shook each of their hands but hesitated when she got to Daniel.

"I'm going to take Beatrice out for ice cream. Maybe we'll see you all again soon," she waved, then placed her hand on her daughter's back and guided her away from the group. As she left, Auryn could hear her mother whisper, "What's wrong with your other friends?" She watched Beatrice shrink a little as they disappeared from view.

Beatrice fidgeted nervously in the car. Nothing was wrong with Auryn or any of her other friends, she knew that. So why was her mother acting this way?

"I hope you know I invited Claire along with us," her mother told her, interrupting the spiral of worry Beatrice found herself falling into.

That's fine, she thought, she hadn't seen Claire in a bit, not since she had been sitting with Auryn. "Oh, cool!" she replied.

Her mother parked the car outside Claire's house and Beatrice smiled as her friend flung open the back door and hugged her tightly.

"So happy to see you. I've missed you. It's been a while, hasn't it?" Claire laughed, pulling away and buckling her seatbelt.

"Yeah, it's so good to see you," Beatrice grinned, "I'm excited to hang out."

They made it to the ice cream place, ordered 3 cones and took a table outside to watch the sunset.

"So…how were tryouts?" Claire asked.

"Really good, I think Auryn and I are gonna get in!" Beatrice instantly brightened.

"Oooh, who's Auryn?" she asked with excitement.

"She's new. I asked her to tryout with me so I wouldn't be as lonely. I really think you'd like her!" Beatrice had always been a friendly person and it made her so happy to think about her two friends meeting and getting to know each other.

Her mother interjected, "Now, Beatrice, why don't we talk about something else. We don't want Claire thinking she's not your best friend."

Beatrice knew how her mother was but was still a bit shocked. Claire would always be her best friend. She shook her head, "But she is my best friend, Mom. I don't want you to compare them like that. All I wanted was for her to meet Auryn."

Her mother blinked, Bea seemed upset, "Well, I just didn't want Claire feeling bad," she replied defensively.

"Would it be cool if I sat with you tomorrow?" Claire asked, then added, "I missed you, Bea."

"I missed you too. That'd be fun. Let's do it!"

As Beatrice made her way home, she bit her lip in anxiety. Was she really as bad a friend as her mother was saying? She had just wanted Auryn to meet Claire. That wasn't wrong at all, it was her mother who had made her feel bad. Even though she didn't mean to hurt her feelings, what she said made Beatrice doubt herself. She wished she could understand and carried that feeling with her into the evening and as she fell asleep that night.

THE GATHERING

Auryn sat at the lunch table with Daniel, Lena, and Emma. They were minding their own business. This made it oddly silent, since the usually talkative Daniel was buckled down with homework he didn't get done the night before. As Auryn nibbled her sandwich, she noticed Beatrice walking in with a taller, brown-haired girl.

"Hey, Auryn! I really wanted you to meet Claire. She's my childhood friend," Beatrice had a big smile on her face.

Auryn held out her hand, which Claire quickly took, "Hi! It's really nice to meet you! This is Daniel, Emma and Lena!"

The three popped up at the mention of their names, giving small waves as Auryn introduced them.

"I'm grabbing lunch, you coming, Bea?" Claire asked.

Beatrice took a seat, "I'll catch up with you."

Claire shrugged and walked to the lunch line while Beatrice looked at Auryn.

"Last night, my mom compared Claire to you. It made me feel like a bad friend for wanting you to meet her. I feel like I'm doing everything wrong," Beatrice blurted, but quiet enough for only Auryn to hear.

Auryn nodded understandingly despite, well, not understanding. She tried to appear confident so as not to deter Beatrice. "I'm really sorry. I'm always here to listen to what you have to say."

Beatrice smiled, "Thanks. I just want her to understand that I love all my friends, especially Claire."

"I hear you. I'm sorry, Bea," Auryn stated softly. Beatrice blinked in surprise. She wasn't used to being listened to so fully. She realized it was amazing to feel safe enough to tell these things to Auryn.

"Can I offer something to think about?" Auryn asked, receiving a nod.

"It's okay to want to introduce your friends to me, but I think your mom just didn't want Claire getting the wrong idea. Even if she didn't say it in a way that helped you understand, you aren't doing anything wrong, Bea," Auryn again used the nickname she had heard Claire use for her, which made Beatrice smile.

"It's like she doesn't understand how it affects me!" Beatrice replied.

Auryn took Beatrice's hand and looked her in the eyes, "I'm sorry Bea. I can see how that makes you feel," she was familiar with the emotion, just not being caused by a parent.

"Thanks, Auryn, you know just what to say." Beatrice had a smile on her face as Claire made her way back to the table. She sat down next to Beatrice and handed her a bag of chips.

"I figured you weren't coming, but I didn't want you going hungry," Claire joked.

"Oh, thanks!" Beatrice smiled, popping the bag open.

They slipped into a comfortable silence. It was interrupted by the sound of a book slamming shut.

"Done!" Daniel announced, sliding his books and papers into his bag.

Lena gave him a thumbs up, "That was a difficult assignment. Next time we could study together."

Emma nodded, "I do take some mean notes, I could join."

Claire turned her head to Auryn, "You guys just met and started to sit together, huh?"

"Yep," Auryn replied.

She continued, "Some of the girls at the table I used to sit at talked about it. Now that you have a table, some girls had to move to my old one."

"Are they upset?" Daniel chimed in.

"Kind of irritated, but I really wouldn't worry," Claire sighed.

Daniel made eye contact with Emma, exchanging anxious glances.

Auryn placed her hand on Emma's, "Nothing bad is gonna happen, I promise."

Emma replied with a soft smile and nod. Daniel seemed to reciprocate the calm feeling.

"I think it's cool you guys got your own table. Kind of like a cool new group or something," Claire commented.

The statement made Auryn perk up, "Is that how groups form?"

"Sometimes, yeah. Honestly, I really don't know how they form, they've just been there."

Auryn listened intently, abandoning her food, "That's really interesting, actually. I never really understood how and why these separate groups form."

Emma perked up, "Really?"

"It just doesn't make sense why everyone isn't friends with everyone," Auryn said.

"This school is a lot bigger than your old one, Auryn," Daniel replied.

"We had groups, but it was still like we were one big group because we were all still friends," she stated.

As lunchtime came to a close, Auryn stood up, "Can we all get together this weekend? It can be at my house."

Daniel and Emma were the first to confirm, then Lena and Beatrice. Claire hesitated. "Am I invited too?"

"Of course! If you want to come, I'd love to have you." Auryn and Claire exchanged numbers before going to class.

"I invited my friends over this weekend, is that okay?" Auryn asked her Father as they lounged in the living room. She was on the floor, arms stretched upwards.

"More than okay, you know I'd love to meet them,"

he smiled, watching the light from the windows highlight her face.

"Awesome, because they're part of my big plan. I wanna help them, not just them though, the whole school!"

He tried to make himself look calm and collected. Truthfully, he was starting to grow more concerned, but knew Auryn couldn't see it. "It's just like you to see the best in everyone. Do you want to tell me more?"

"There's so much I could say, I want to inspire everyone, I want them to embrace themselves and feel safe enough to do it!"

Her Father simply nodded, letting her speak about whatever her mind thought up. He loved hearing everything she had to talk about and would let her do so undeterred. This had never backfired. Even if he felt her goals and pace were too big and fast, he was certain she'd find her way.

"When I get them together this weekend, that'll really kick everything into motion, I'm sure of it."

He loved how certain she was, how brightly she smiled. She saw the world in such an optimistic light. But there was no denying there was also a sense of fear. His concern was, what if this backfires and her beautiful optimism is shattered?

Even strong fathers have their doubts, but he knew if he kept faith in what he had taught her since the day she was born, Auryn would be okay in the end. Her strong sense of self and powerful empathy served as a promise, assuring him that she was kind, caring, and brave enough to pick herself up after a fall—although he knew he'd never let her stray too far.

"Thank you," Auryn said, her eyes now looking into his.

"For what?" her Father asked, he hadn't done anything out of the ordinary.

"For moving. It's like the universe knew I needed something new in my life too!" the grin on her face made him soften.

"Good things are coming our way, I know it, Auryn."

As her friends arrived one by one, Auryn was thrilled. She could finally set her plan in action, the one that had been forming in her head and she had been endlessly jotting down since she came to the new school.

They lay in a circle on the floor of her bedroom. Auryn wasn't moving, just laying on her back, as a question occurred to her.

"If you weren't scared of what people thought, what would you do?"

Daniel was the first to speak up, "I think I'd come out to the whole school."

Auryn smiled, "How would that feel?"

"Really good! I think after that I'd feel really confident."

"What about the rest of you?"

Claire sat up. "I'd run track."

"I'd love it if you'd join the team!" Lena stated excitedly.

Claire looked down at her legs, "Yeah, but I don't want kids to make fun of my body."

"I'm sorry, Claire. Kids really do that?" Auryn asked, now sitting up too. Feeling more motivated than ever, she asked, "What would it feel like if they weren't like that?"

"I can't imagine. I guess I'd be really motivated," Claire smiled.

The group went around talking about what they'd do and stating how confident and empowered they'd feel. Auryn loved it but was mindful of containing her excitement to keep the focus on them. She simply kept asking questions and allowed them to speak.

"What if we could make it happen?" Auryn asked, glancing excitedly at each of her friends.

"What do you mean?" Beatrice asked, holding onto her pillow.

"I mean, if we could help people feel safe enough to be themselves, so much could be changed."

"How could we do that though?" Emma asked, rocking back and forth.

"We have to be the first. If we show people we're unafraid, I think it could be really inspiring," Auryn said. She pulled a pad of paper out from under her bed.

"But how would I ever tell my parents I want to do track?" Claire asked. "They're so busy all the time. I'd bother them. And what if they thought I couldn't do it?"

"I'm sorry you feel like that, Claire," Auryn rested her hand on Claire's shoulder, "the goal is to inspire people. It might be confusing or scary when you start, but once you develop self-confidence, won't they be happy for you?"

"I think your parents would really admire you trying new things, Claire," Daniel offered, trying to gently encourage her.

Claire smiled. "I think your parents would admire your bravery if you came out to them," she told Daniel.

"See, what if everyone could have these thoughts about everyone?" Auryn surveyed her friends' faces, finding them smiling and looking to her too.

"I think that'd be awesome, Auryn!" Beatrice spoke, her face full of optimism. Auryn couldn't help but share that exhilarating feeling.

Emma piped up, "We're with you!"

At school the following week, Lena sighed as she caught up to Daniel in the hallway. She didn't even greet him, just gave a half-hearted wave. Were Mondays always this tiring?

"Hard morning?" Daniel asked, a half smile on his face.

"Just tired," Lena groaned.

Daniel chuckled and the two walked in silence. Before they arrived at Lena's classroom, she spoke again, "Why don't we go sit down in my first class until school starts?"

He gave a quick nod and the two ducked into her classroom. As they made their way to open desks, Daniel seemed startled. Lena decided not to ask about it until they were both seated.

"Is something wrong?" Lena asked, tapping him on the shoulder to get his attention.

"Nothing…nothing really," Daniel said, his eyes not moving to look at Lena.

She followed his gaze to a kid sitting at his desk drawing. It clicked in her mind and she turned to Daniel.

"You want to talk to Joey!" She raised her hand to point at the kid in question. Before her arm was even extended for a second, Daniel snatched it down.

"Shhh! I…I don't know if I'm ready, Lena," he mumbled.

She gave him a quick nudge, "Isn't part of Auryn's plan to be yourself? I can help you, ya know."

Daniel turned to Lena. He bit his lip in worry and his eyes darted around the wall behind her. Lena simply took his hand, "Don't worry, we can do this."

As he was about to answer, a voice from where Joey was sitting interrupted the conversation.

"What are you *wearing*?"

A boy Lena didn't recognize was sitting behind Joey. He pinched and grabbed at the fabric of the floral-patterned shirt Joey was wearing over his normal white one.

"Isn't this a girl's shirt?" The boy asked again and snickered.

Joey didn't say anything, just spun the pencil he held in his hands. Lena looked to Daniel and the two stood up, instantly making their way to the scene. Daniel observed that the other kids in the classroom were keeping to themselves, not doing anything to stop it. It made him upset. Auryn was right, he thought, why don't the kids here feel compelled to help?

"Why do you care?" Lena was the first to speak up. Her arms were folded and she was full of attitude. Daniel watched her, but he was worried that her aggressive demeanor wasn't the right way to handle the situation.

"It's not his fault that you have something against his clothing," Daniel spoke, his voice full of confidence. It made Lena drop her defensive position, a smile rising on her face.

"Whatever. I don't have time for this," the boy let go and walked off. As Daniel glanced around the room, he noticed some kids smiling and some even looking up at him. He placed a hand on Joey's shoulder. "If you ever need us, you know where to find us, okay?"

"I like your shirt!" Lena exclaimed, waving as she walked back with Daniel.

Joey simply gave a nod and a small "thank you" before looking down again.

"Maybe that's all he's ready for," Daniel murmured as he went back to their spot.

The two made small conversation. Lena sat on the classroom table near the front row while Daniel drew on the whiteboard. Their conversation was cut short when Auryn poked her head in the door.

"I knew I'd find you here!" She grinned, skipping toward them.

Daniel gave Auryn a hug before going back to his drawing. "It's good to see you, Auryn," he said, a satisfied smile still on his face.

"What's he so happy about?" Auryn asked Lena, genuine curiosity on her face.

"He stood up for someone today," Lena grinned.

"You did? Daniel, I'm so proud of you!" Auryn smiled as Daniel turned around.

"Thanks. I really felt motivated to help," Daniel sat in the chair near the table.

"Did you feel better when you did it?" Auryn asked.

"I felt really confident, and really strong," Daniel replied, pride showing on his face.

"That's awesome," Auryn gave him a high five.

"It made me so mad. I wanted to kick him!" Lena grumbled.

"I'm sorry you got angry," Auryn's voice tried to soothe her. "Why do you think you got mad?"

"I can't fix it, ya know?" Lena clenched her fists.

"I hear you," Auryn said empathetically.

Joey looked up. Despite the chatter of the other students in the room, Lena thought he was paying attention to their conversation.

"Do you want to come over here?" Auryn asked. She had followed Lena's gaze.

"C'mon, Joey! It's okay," Lena waved to him.

Joey shyly got up and took the chair next to Daniel.

"What do you think you could do to fix it, Lena?" Auryn asked, continuing their conversation.

"I don't know!" Lena shouted. Her voice startled her. She hadn't meant to be that loud.

"Are you okay?" Auryn asked.

Lena shook her head, "My dad does things like this to my mom and it makes me hate him!" She slammed her fist on the table.

"Hey, hey, I'm so sorry, Lena," Auryn put her hand on Lena's shoulder, "I'm really sorry."

Lena didn't answer, she simply fell into a hug with Auryn, who gently soothed her. When she pulled back, Auryn simply asked, "What do you need?"

"I just want a space to feel safe enough to talk about it. You helped me out with that, thank you," Lena gave a tearful smile.

"I'm so thankful you told us, Lena. Processing your emotions is good, I'm sorry you're afraid to let yourself feel."

By now, the few kids who had come into the room before class were staring at their group, but nobody in the group was focused on that, their only focus was the conversation.

The bell rang, signaling lunch. Auryn and Emma filed out of their classroom and headed to the cafeteria. After getting their food, they met the rest of their group at the table. The first to greet them was Lena, then Daniel, then Beatrice and Claire, who came together.

"I want to hang out again this weekend. Would any of you want to bring a friend?" Auryn looked from one friend to another.

It was almost a unanimous "Sure!" Of course her friends wouldn't mind adding to the group. But Emma stayed silent, small strands of hair falling over her face.

"I'm not sure, I don't have any other friends," she almost whispered.

Auryn patted her back gently, "It's okay, Emma. I really appreciate you being honest. If you change your mind, can you tell me?"

Emma nodded before turning her attention back to her food.

"I can send out a group text," Auryn suggested, "are you all free this weekend?"

"I was wondering when you would suggest that," Claire giggled, "thanks for helping me feel so welcome with all of you!"

"It's awesome to have you with us, Claire," Daniel told her, "I'll ask my parents, could we meet at my house?"

"I'd really like to see your house, Daniel," Beatrice told him, leaning forward.

"They're kind of uptight. I hope you don't mind," he sheepishly admitted.

"Don't worry about it, Daniel," Auryn replied, "I'm thankful you offered your house."

Auryn didn't know how they were able to fit almost ten people into Daniel's father's SUV, but somehow they did. Daniel brought Joey, Beatrice brought Claire, and Lena brought a friend Auryn hadn't met. She introduced herself as Amelia and Auryn recognized her from the table of popular girls.

Auryn hadn't brought anyone and neither had Emma. That didn't bother Auryn at all. She reached into her bag and pulled out one of her notebooks, in which she had jotted down little ideas. Her eyes scanned the words until she found what she was looking for, a small passage detailing her plans for the get-together. As she was about to read them, Daniel's father spoke up.

"It sure doesn't seem like you all just met," he joked. Auryn smiled.

Claire spoke first, "You can thank Auryn for that! She's really good at bringing people together!" Claire was sitting next to Auryn and gave her a thankful glance, brightening Auryn's already excited smile.

Beatrice chimed in, "She's really unapologetically herself, it's inspiring." Beatrice was in the row of seats behind Auryn. She leaned on the seat in front of her so Auryn could see her face, which was spread in a wide smile.

"That's really nice, Auryn." Daniel's father smiled.

"Thanks, Daniel's dad," she joked.

"Oh please, you can just call me Noah," he chuckled, but then lost his smile as his eyes made contact with the road again. Noah knit his brows in thought. He could see the anxiety in these kids, but when Auryn was around they felt really inspired to be themselves. He had never met Auryn before, but he could feel her carefree energy in the way she expressed herself.

The car pulled to a stop in front of a moderately-sized house. Auryn admired all the flowers in front.

"Your house looks really nice, Daniel," Emma said, hopping out of the car.

Daniel, who had taken the passenger's side, walked next to her, "Thanks, my only worry is how I'm gonna fit everyone in my room."

"Can we make space in the living room," Joey suggested, walking up from behind Daniel.

Beatrice nodded, "Maybe a huge blanket fort!"

The other kids piped up in agreement, and Noah laughed, "You can do whatever you want as long as the house is clean when you leave it." He gave Daniel a knowing look and stated under his breath, "We don't want mom to be upset."

Noah unlocked the door to the house, letting everyone stream in. He simply watched them, feeling a change in the way his son was acting. Daniel was so confident with all these new people, it was nice to see.

DANIEL'S STRUGGLE

After a quick tour of their options, the group decided to make a cozy space for themselves on the floor in Daniel's basement. It was a pretty wide-open space, so Auryn and her friends had no trouble setting up.

"Does anyone want snacks? I can make that happen," Daniel suggested.

The group nodded in agreement which sent Daniel hopping up the stairs and into the kitchen. Opening the cabinet, he started to grab chips, popcorn, and anything crunchy he could find. He was almost done when his father entered the room, looking apprehensive.

"Dad?" Daniel asked tentatively as Noah took a seat at the table. He focused his attention on his hands.

"I keep hearing you mention a plan with Auryn. What's going on? Do you want to tell me what it's about?"

Daniel nodded, set the bags down and sat across from his father before excitedly sharing, "Auryn wants us all to feel more self-confident and safe enough to express who we truly are, so we're gonna lead by example and show that we're capable!"

Noah carefully watched Daniel and bit his lip in worry. Despite the fact that Daniel had not told him directly, he knew his son was gay. He just didn't know if he was ready to accept the reality of it, let alone how he would handle it.

After a minute with no response, Daniel asked, "Is that okay, Dad?" He looked at him with anxiety in his expression.

"Yeah-Yeah, don't worry about it," Noah replied, waving a hand dismissively. But this didn't convince Daniel, who quickly stood up to gather more snacks.

Daniel spent his life trying to please his father, to be the son his father wanted him to be. Caving, he offered a solution which he thought would make his father happy, "Auryn and Beatrice are cheerleaders, so maybe I could do a sport to be closer to them." Daniel hoped his voice didn't reveal the dread he felt at that suggestion.

His father instantly brightened, "I think that'd be a great idea."

Daniel was used to this kind of delicate dance with his father. It was the only way he could feel safe. Well at least his father felt better, he assured himself, even if he didn't.

Daniel bundled up his snacks and walked down the stairs, then dropped them in the center of their little area. He sat down and brought his knees up to his chest.

He felt confident he could come out at school—the thought once terrified him, now it filled him with hope.

He figured that maybe once he came out, he could meet other kids like him. But that thought quickly disappeared as another came screeching in and made his stomach twist in fear: What would happen when his parents found out? Surely, they'd be upset, maybe frustrated, or worse? He didn't know.

Daniel felt the group's eyes on him. When he looked up, they were looking at him intently. The fear and confusion must have shown on his face.

"Daniel?" Auryn asked, concerned.

"Yeah?"

"Is everything okay?"

Daniel flushed from the attention, everyone seemed to be focused on him. "Yeah-Yeah, I'm fine."

"Would you tell me if you weren't?" Auryn asked, trying not to pressure him.

Daniel nodded and the group resumed talking. Auryn could see there hadn't been a change in his body language. He still seemed to be struggling. When she was certain the rest of the group wasn't paying attention, she again shifted her focus to Daniel. He caught her eye and she gestured to another room. The two walked out and the rest of the group didn't seem to mind.

Auryn knew it was important to do her best to help Daniel feel okay. Putting him on the spot in front of a lot of people wasn't the best way to handle things. After Beatrice's mother and small outbursts from Lena about her father, Auryn started to get the sense that parents had a big part to play in how her friends expressed themselves. Just because she had been fostered in an environment full of safety and security didn't mean her friends had. It made her heart ache to know her friends didn't feel that same safety and security. While she didn't understand everything, she was determined to try.

"Are you able to tell me?" Auryn asked him, closing the door.

"It's my parents..." Daniel was holding back and Auryn let him, knowing she'd ease it out over time.

"I'm really sorry," Auryn replied

"It's not a big deal."

"It doesn't seem that way, Daniel," Auryn persisted.

"I know." On one hand, Daniel wanted to tell Auryn everything—he always felt safe enough to do that with her and nothing was different about that now. But on the other hand, he was worried that he needed to hold back because of his parents.

"My dad was acting funny and I don't know what I did wrong to make him feel that way."

"I'm really sorry," Auryn said. "It sounds like you feel responsible, but I don't see how you could be."

"Thank you, Auryn," Daniel said, appreciative of her listening.

"Is there a reason why you haven't told your parents?" she asked.

"They know I'm gay, or I think they do, and they're holding back. I really don't want to upset them any further."

Before meeting her new friends, Auryn wouldn't

have had a clue about any of this. Her home community wasn't half as hostile as the one she had now entered, but she was getting the hang of things here the best she could. The only thing she could remember that reminded her of her new friends was her Mother's uncertainty and hesitance. But even in those times, her Father was always there to comfort and assure.

Her friends felt safe around her, Auryn could sense it without having to say a word. But it was practically effortless for her, she had been raised that way. Her Father and Mother set an example for her, which she followed naturally since it had been a part of her forever.

Auryn snapped back to reality, "I'm sorry Daniel. Is there anything else you want to tell me?"

Daniel nodded, "I'm scared they won't love me if I tell them I'm gay. I'm afraid to tell them anything. They say I should just be happy, so I pretend I'm okay."

"Afraid?" Auryn asked, "What does that look like?"

That was something Daniel had never thought of before. He always said whatever he needed to so the people around him would be okay with who he was. He had tried to reach out in the past, but never felt like he was heard or he mattered. His breathing quickened as tears welled in his eyes.

"Daniel? How do you feel?" Auryn asked, bringing him back.

"Sad and alone..." Daniel replied, clenching his fists, "I hate feeling this way!" He let himself cry, "I hate feeling at all!"

Auryn knew that saying anything wouldn't help, she just had to be there for her friend. She opened her arms and let Daniel cry into them.

"Daniel?" His sobs were interrupted by the voice of Claire. The group peered into the room, called over by the sound of his crying.

Everyone felt what Daniel was feeling. It was uncomfortable, but Auryn role-modeled bravery and they followed her lead. Gathering around Daniel, everyone sat down to let him release his pain. He continued to cry into Auryn. Some of his friends cried silently too. They could all feel the love and acceptance Auryn was spreading, without even saying a word.

They watched Auryn nurture him, rubbing his back and affirming his sadness. She only said, "I hear you," and, "it's okay to feel."

Auryn wasn't trying to fix it, telling him not to care, to stay positive, or to ignore what others thought. She didn't tell him how or what to feel. She just let him feel. This amazed the group. They felt worthy, like they could express their feelings too. Feeling this was freedom, it felt good to let out the bad.

When Daniel came out of the embrace, he looked at all his friends, they were dazed. Suddenly, a big smile came onto his face and he began laughing. The air was heavy with sadness, but his laugh pierced through it. It was a small chuckle at first, then a few more laughs, then the entire group was laughing. No real words had been spoken for a while, not even Auryn's assuring ones, and yet they were laughing.

While they laughed, Noah peered into the room. He was worried about how to approach everyone when they were so closely knit.

Daniel saw him and jumped in almost instantly, "Hi Dad! We were just talking about stuff we liked."

Noah didn't really seem to believe him, but he let it slide.

"Is that okay, Dad?" Daniel asked.

"Yeah-Yeah!" Noah replied, "I just wanted to see what was going on."

"It's okay, you can stay if you want." The group resumed their original seats in the other room as Daniel offered up the idea.

Daniel's fear and hesitance around his father was new to Auryn. While he showed that fear when he first met her, he had been really quick to warm up. But when he was around his father, he was like a different person. This compelled Auryn to want to protect him, she was sure her Father would frown upon it though. Her Mother had tried to shield her from the bad before and it made her feel helpless. She didn't want that for Daniel.

"C'mon Daniel, does your dad really want to hang out with us?" Lena joked.

That made Noah snap back to reality, "Don't worry about me, I just wanted to make sure everything was okay." Seemingly uncomfortable, he was halfway up the stairs before he said, "You kids call me if you need anything."

As he left, Lena looked at Auryn and snickered, "Looks like you aren't used to some of that parent stuff, Auryn." Lena knew the awkwardness with her parents all too well. When her father wasn't yelling, he was avoiding her and her mother, so whenever they talked it was super awkward.

Auryn opened her mouth to reply, but Daniel spoke.

"I'm sorry about my dad. I guess he just wants me to be happy," he shrugged, looking anxious.

"I know you feel bad, Daniel, and I'm sorry too, but why is he worried about your happiness? I don't understand."

He shrugged yet again, "I guess I'm worried too."

Auryn felt concerned for her friends and wanted to remove the oppressive atmosphere, it felt like it was going to crush them all.

"We have a lot of work cut out for us, but thankfully we're here together!" Auryn grabbed her notebook with the little notes and doodles of all her big plans.

"Who wants to be happy?" she asked, eyes bright with excitement.

"We do!" Her friends yelled, then giggled at one another when they noticed they had chanted in sync.

This made Auryn laugh too, "How about being free and having fun?" she managed between giggles.

"We do!" they said in sync again.

"Let's think of one thing each, one thing that we want to do to express ourselves."

Over the course of a few hours, they had encouraged everyone to find one thing to do. Lena decided on becoming better at track, she'd ignore the mean kids and run to her heart's content. Beatrice wanted to become a member of the student senate. She was social and wanted to help make change, so she was thrilled to work on her student council campaign. Daniel had a much smaller goal; he had hidden a pink button-up in his room and wanted to wear it to school. He loved how it looked but was worried he'd be made fun of. Claire wanted to encourage other people to join them, so she'd look around for more friends.

The rest of the group followed suit, delivering their plans. Auryn showed support, but she didn't ask questions, only listened. She was so thrilled that she bounced in her seat. Her friends meant the world to her and she knew this new group made her friends feel the same.

They all lay on the floor silently setting out their own strategies. Auryn smiled at the thought of what they were going to do. She had already helped a bit, but she was 100% certain that, despite the bumps in the road, they'd accomplish great things—they just needed to stick together.

Her Father should know about all this, he deserved to. He was so kind and thoughtful, and his gentle encouragement always made Auryn feel loved and safe.

"Do you need me, Auryn?" the voice of her Father

rang through the room. She sat up, she couldn't see him, but she felt him. The other kids didn't seem to stir.

"I was hoping you'd appear," she brought her knees to her chest.

"What's on your mind?" he asked encouragingly, "I'm here."

He was always there for Auryn. Wherever she was, he was there with his comforting presence.

"You're always there for me, Father," she smiled.

"Always and Forever," he replied.

"I wish my friends had a parent like you."

"What makes you say that?"

"They seem to have such a complicated relationship with their parents. Why can't it be easy? They act so different around their parents."

"What do you mean by that?"

"I don't know for sure, but they're holding back. There's so much they want to be, so much they want to say, but they don't. Are they afraid?"

"How can I support you?" he asked her.

"Tell me what to do. Tell me how to help!"

He was caught off guard. She had never asked to be told what to do. He was concerned she was straying from her true self. Would this worry her Mother? "I know better than that, Auryn," he laughed, "you are smart and compassionate. You might not know now, but the answer will come to you. And no matter what, I'm with you." He found her questions disheartening but remained calm.

"Always and forever?"

"Always and Forever," he replied with love. He let the worries of her Mother leave his head, knowing Auryn's sense of self would prevail.

Auryn closed her eyes and let the guiding voice of her Father leave her head, making it clear enough to drift off. She was filled with a new hope.

THE DESCENT

By the time Monday morning rolled around, Auryn's head was filled with a myriad of thoughts. As the fog of sleep fully cleared, her mind focused on Daniel. She observed him hiding himself from his father. While not physically, he mentally kept a distance and it was almost as if his father could tell. This brought the parent question to her head, why do kids hide who they are from their parents? If they were themselves, wouldn't their parents love them even more? It felt like as long as Daniel hid, his father was fine with him. That wasn't fair! Maybe that was all anyone knew. Maybe everyone was pretending. Maybe everyone had similar struggles. Maybe everyone could relate. Maybe everyone was trapped—even parents!

She wondered then if parents hid their true selves from their children and from each other. If that was the case, no wonder they needed their kids to be a certain way, it's the only way they knew—it's like survival, so of course, any change would feel threatening. This was an explosive discovery!

Auryn knew they all wanted to be free. Was the whole world trapped? How could she right the whole world?

I can't do it all myself, she told herself. And as her Father would say, baby steps. If she took too much on and moved too fast, she'd risk falling. But the thought that everyone was struggling aided her quest.

She tried to untangle the knots in her head, she'd overwhelm herself otherwise and that wasn't her goal. Her notebook was filled with pages of notes detailing the events that came into her head. Was she done? Now that she had everyone gathered, she could start encouraging her friends and make real changes.

When her Father called her to the car to head to school, she was ready for anything, especially bringing her plan to life. During the drive, she bounced with excitement, daydreaming about everything that was to come. When they arrived, she hopped out of the car and skipped toward the building.

As she approached the courtyard, Auryn saw a crowd of people gathered. Glancing up, she saw Beatrice alongside Claire. They were handing out small stickers to everyone. It must be her campaign for student council, Auryn thought. Thrilled, she made her way through the group to her friends. The crowd was big, which was a good sign for Bea since she was concerned she wasn't too big among the more "popular" kids.

Getting closer, Auryn heard chanting from the group. She became confused when she read the sticker someone had dropped, "Be me! Be free!" Auryn tensed as the crowd chanted the slogan. She had serious doubts about this and was growing concerned. This was not what she had in mind. Auryn knew encouraging a person to be their authentic self couldn't be a forceful campaign, it took very gentle encouragement and the timing had to be right.

While she had never seen aggressive groups or riots, she knew this wasn't right. It felt almost dangerous. Where had they learned this? Life wasn't a fight or a riot, and neither was being oneself.

The crowd was unfazed by the ringing of the morning bell. Auryn wasn't surprised to see Lena congratulating Beatrice and pulling her into a tight hug. What surprised Auryn was the whispering. Lena muttered something quietly into Beatrice's ear. When she pulled away, Beatrice let out another, "Be me! Be free!"

The crowd pumped their fists and rallied together. Auryn could see Daniel in his pink shirt handing out stickers to kids going by. To the left, Emma spoke with the group of girls she had wanted to be a part of that first day in class. This was amazing but terrifying, Auryn knew it wasn't the right approach.

Shaking her head, she made her way over to Beatrice. Maybe all this was a big misunderstanding, she thought, but she had her doubts. Lena was the first to notice Auryn, her face brightening as she got Beatrice's attention. The two waved her over. "Auryn!" Beatrice called.

"Just so you all know, Auryn is the one responsible for this new change!" Lena happily shared with the crowd, giving Auryn a big smile.

This received a great reaction from the crowd, but Auryn felt her stomach drop. Not like this, she thought, this is all wrong. Beatrice looked like she felt the same way. She looked deflated as the attention shifted to Auryn who then redirected the crowd, "Beatrice is leading the way, go Bea!"

The whoops and cheers finally died down and the crowd went on their way. It was just the three of them now and Beatrice perked up again as best she could.

Am I responsible? Auryn worried. She wasn't used to thinking like this. Maybe if she kept herself quiet, this wouldn't happen again. She must have done something wrong and she felt terrible. As her friends walked away, the voice of her Father called out again, as if he were next to her.

"Be careful, dearest, listen to yourself."

Swallowing hard, she decided to push away his voice. Her Father had never tried to enforce her actions, but his voice sounded worried.

A tap on her shoulder made her realize she had been standing in the courtyard on her own. One of the counselors had come to bring her into the school. Auryn didn't say much, she just anxiously followed him to the office. Her stomach and head fuzzy with worry.

His tone shifted from awkward guidance to a sterner disposition as the two sat down. With his head resting on his hands, he looked to Auryn.

"Did you see what was going on out there?" he raised an eyebrow.

"Beatrice is super excited about running," Auryn suggested. She felt anxious, she'd never been spoken to in that tone before. How could she respond when it felt like he was pointing a finger at her? She shrunk a little, losing her self-confidence in that moment.

"Did you hear what they said about parents and teachers?" This time his voice was even louder and it made Auryn shrink further. Just like her friends, she found herself unable to speak.

She tried to reach for her Father, but in that moment, she was unarmed.

"Well...?" The counselor prodded.

Auryn jolted a little bit and tried to regain herself, forgetting all she knew in that stressful moment. "I don't think I was there long enough."

"Let me explain something to you," he sighed.

While the counselor spoke, Auryn tried to calm herself. Her eyes darted around the office. Despite the motivational quotes and posters, she felt incredibly anxious. When adults talked like this, it made her terrified. This must be why kids feel so afraid. This is why kids are afraid to feel.

"We all want you kids to be able to have fun, but it's like you don't know any better."

What does that even mean, Auryn wondered. She had wanted to be respectful. Even if kids were younger, comments like these made them doubt themselves. Auryn believed that adults genuinely cared. Maybe if they knew what they did wrong they'd want to make amends. The way they spoke and the messages their words conveyed couldn't be intentional, they couldn't mean to say things the way they do…could they?

Although deflated, Auryn kept herself distanced from what the counselor was saying. She just *knew* she wasn't doing anything wrong. She reminded herself that love for one another made the world go around.

Taking a deep breath, Auryn tried to explain. "Where I'm from, kids don't have to fight to be seen by you guys, they—"

"Well of course, that's all we want for kids, Auryn. You just don't listen to us." This clearly didn't sit well with the counselor.

Auryn found this twisted. It was the exact opposite! Adults don't listen to kids—do they even listen to each other?

She found herself swimming in this feeling of anxiety and dread. Auryn didn't like it and she wanted it to go away. So, contrary to her instincts, she decided to try something. "It was my idea, I'm sorry."

The counselor let some tension leave his body, "Don't let it happen again. I'll excuse your first period."

After he allowed her to leave, Auryn stood outside his office for a moment wringing her hands. She felt upset and scared, but believed she needed to keep quiet about it. It felt like the weight of the entire school was on her as she made her way to her second class. The bell rang, signaling a 5-minute break period. Would 5 minutes be enough time to get rid of her negative emotions?

As she sat down, she could hear footsteps running toward her. "Auryn! Hey!"

Beatrice's voice rang shrill in her brain as Auryn looked up to see her accompanied by a large group of friends.

"What happened? Are you okay?" Beatrice asked, practically falling onto the bench next to Auryn.

"Did you tell that counselor person to piss off?" Lena joked, her arms folded.

Auryn opened her mouth to speak but couldn't find the right words. Her eyes darted between Beatrice and Lena, and all the people surrounding them.

"Did we do something wrong?" Beatrice asked, instantly frozen.

This stopped the spiral of emotions Auryn had been feeling. In that moment, she saw the anxious looks on all of their faces.

"No, you didn't do anything. He just wanted to ask me if I was okay since I was lagging behind, that's all."

Lena didn't seem to get it, "That's how they are, they act like they're looking out for you. Don't let them fool you though, you're smart."

Auryn could almost see the pain radiating off Lena, the distrust she had for adults. She tried to sound as loving as she could, pushing through her own pain.

"I hear you, Lena."

Lena softened, "Yeah okay, whatever."

"Why don't we all meet at lunch to celebrate Bea

finally running for student council," Auryn suggested, trying to keep the tone in her voice cheerful.

The group chatted excitedly as they dispersed with the bell. Auryn tried to suppress the feeling of dread that consumed her.

Auryn let herself flop onto the bench, setting her tray on the table and sighing. She had tried to pour more focus into her classwork in order to drown out that feeling of anxiety, but to no avail. Math felt like a second language, she couldn't force herself to focus. As she thought to herself, she took a moment to glance around the room. Her table was unusually empty. She spotted Beatrice and quickly noticed a crowd was gathering.

Letting out another sigh, Auryn stood up. She knew whatever Beatrice was up to, she needed to scope out. It felt like her responsibility.

"Auryn! Hey!" Beatrice waved her over, "I was waiting for you!"

Auryn gave her a small smile, "Why did you need me?"

Beatrice took her hand and pulled her up onto a bench so they could stand above the group of kids.

"I made all the announcements. I just wanted to see you."

Auryn shifted her gaze to the crowd of students who were beginning to chat among themselves. With the pep rally in two weeks, she was sure Bea had a plan and she wanted to hear all about it.

"Thank you for listening everyone! I hope to speak with you all again soon."

The students dispersed back to their tables and Auryn and Beatrice met up with their friends at their usual table. There were a few new faces.

"How was everyone today? What did I miss? Fill me in," Auryn smiled genuinely for the first time today.

"Well, you know what I'm up to!" Beatrice grinned.

"I was interviewing the crowd this morning!" Emma bounced, "I might start doing some video interviews for Beatrice's campaign. I love this whole reporter thing! When my parents watch the news, they're always so glued. Maybe they'll watch me this time."

"Wow!" Auryn replied, "I'm proud of you."

While she hadn't known Emma much longer than her other friends, Auryn had watched Emma transition from a shy, lonely girl to an outgoing kid with a vision. It was truly inspiring.

"What about you, Daniel?" Auryn turned to him.

"Well…" Daniel started, sheepishly scratching the back of his head, "I designed Bea's stickers! It was really fun to play with the fonts and stuff."

"They are really cool!" Beatrice spoke up. "Thanks, Daniel."

"Well, duh, I enjoyed it," he laughed. "Also, I've been in my new shirt all day! I only got compliments, nobody said anything rude." His blue eyes sparkled.

"I'm so glad," Auryn gave him a pat on the

shoulder.

He continued, "It felt like everyone saw the real me, not some mask I've been putting on."

Claire was the next to pipe up, "Beatrice made me her campaign manager."

"You know Beatrice the best, I don't think anyone could do it better!" Auryn grinned.

The only one not speaking up was Lena. She had her arms folded and eyes averted. Auryn reached past Daniel to give her a small tap.

"You did a good job today too. You kept Beatrice safe in case anyone would have said harmful things."

Lena smiled, "Okay, whatever."

Auryn accepted the answer. She knew Lena was only being shy. It would take time for Lena to open up and trust the other kids. Things had been moving so fast.

"You seem preoccupied, Auryn. Are you alright?" The voice of her Father came again, she felt herself drifting from the table.

"I'm not so sure I am. Something happened and I'm not sure what to do. I upset the guidance counselor."

"Tell me more," he encouraged her to keep opening up.

"Well…when I got to school and into the courtyard there was a big rally for Beatrice, since she's running for student council. They were chanting 'Be free! Be me!' and then the counselor—"

While she shared all this, her Father didn't speak, only listened.

"He made me feel terrible, he was talking like he was all torn!"

"What do you mean by that?" he asked.

"He said he was supportive, but at the same time he wasn't. I felt uncomfortable. I felt like my friends, like I had to hide myself!" She had never felt these feelings before. Sure, everyone felt sad, but she had never felt so unseen or helpless and she didn't like it. Tears began to well up in her eyes.

"I'm sorry, Auryn." He knew there was no risk that she would lose herself, his teachings were rooted in her and who she was.

"I feel responsible. I need to turn it around, I didn't mean to mess it up!"

"Do you believe that it was you who caused your friends to act this way…in a way that you don't even understand?"

"No…I-I guess not."

"Why would you want to do this to your friends?"

"I would never!"

"But you feel responsible?"

While Auryn's Mother was usually silent, comfortable in his guidance, her voice drowned his out, reaching for her child.

"I'm sorry, Auryn, we can fix this, you can fix this."

Auryn knew her Mother, she could be apprehensive and timid, uncertain of the world around her.

"Thank you, Mother, I can fix this, I know it."

Auryn had the gut feeling that her Mother was out to protect her, it was a promise deep within her. She wanted to encourage her friends in a better way, without fighting. Disrespecting adults wasn't the way, leading by example was.

When we show parents and teachers how freeing it is to embrace and accept ourselves, then maybe a better future can be worked toward for all of us. It isn't something to fight for, it's something to demonstrate. She thought of how Daniel had to wear a mask to be seen by his parents and how Lena's parents reacted with anger instead of empathy.

"I'm sorry, Father, but Mother is right, I need to fix this."

The voice did not answer.

"Hello? Earth to Auryn?" Beatrice waved her hand over Auryn's face. Her friends were all gazing at her as well.

"Sorry, I-I guess I zoned out," Auryn wiped a stray tear, she was still in the lunchroom.

Her friends resumed their conversation while she looked down at her hands.

"Maybe we could all meet at my house again?" she suggested.

She wasn't met with an answer. Beatrice seemed preoccupied, talking to a group of kids with Claire. Auryn thought she spoke loud enough, but it didn't seem like anybody could hear her.

"Joey and I are setting up a new Dungeons and Dragons campaign with a few people this weekend, but I told my dad we were working on a project so he wouldn't interrupt us," Daniel told Lena.

"Good, honestly I think they'd spoil it if they knew," Lena laughed.

Auryn didn't know how she felt about that, but before she could speak, Emma spoke.

"When I told my parents I wanted to be a reporter, my dad said they don't make a lot of money and that I need to do something else. But when I thought of what Auryn said, I knew I could! So, I just said it was an idea, and they felt better," Auryn knew she needed to help them stay strong.

"I think your parents want the best for you. It's good to tell them the truth," Auryn didn't like telling them what to do or making demands, but she felt cornered.

"No way! They don't understand, Auryn, they don't get it," Lena tried to explain.

"My mom said she didn't want me to get my hopes up in case I don't win the campaign," Beatrice admitted, the group she was talking to had moved on.

Auryn was thoughtful, "Maybe she didn't mean it that way. I know we think they don't understand, but they just want us to feel good! I know it. When we show them that being ourselves feels good and is safe to do, they'll have to know it's okay somewhere deep inside of them."

The group exuded optimism in that moment, despite what they previously believed was true of their parents. They knew their parents loved them, but they wanted to be accepted—even for their flaws—and they hoped it could finally happen.

"Can we meet at my house tomorrow? I want to make a plan for the pep rally. I want to show the other students we can do it," Auryn suggested, it seemed this time she was heard.

"I think that'd be a great idea," Daniel spoke.

"We can join together. We can show the parents and teachers who we really are!" Auryn cheered.

Claire opened her mouth to speak, but soon groups of kids had overheard Auryn's last statement and were gathering to hear more.

Beatrice took Claire's hand and, despite the signs posted all over the lunchroom, stood up on the table.

"Who wants to be free to be themselves! Let's show the world how amazing we are!" Beatrice shouted.

With a final cheer, the crowd dispersed with the bell. Auryn and her friends followed the flow of students to their next class.

"What an awesome week!" Beatrice flopped down onto her makeshift bed on the floor of Auryn's room.

Her friends were in their comfortable clothing, each one had a small pile of blankets and pillows to lean on. Despite her Mother and Father's opposing stances, they agreed to give her space to be with her friends.

"Yeah," Daniel replied, "so many of my new friends can't wait to get involved."

"Everyone is so excited. I've been interviewing so many people and they trust us!" Emma interjected, her face glowing.

"How do you think the pep rally should go?" Auryn asked, looking to Beatrice.

"Claire and I were thinking that getting some people to speak about their dreams and inspirations would be a fun idea."

"Maybe we could encourage more kids to join in by doing that," Claire added, "like in the lunchroom. When we start it, more kids join in."

"I like that idea!" Auryn replied.

"It's like showing adults that we can be different, but still get along," Lena suggested, "they won't have a choice but to accept it!"

By Lena's tone, Auryn could sense that she was all in. Auryn was warming up to the idea.

"How could we get more parents to come to the rally?" Emma asked, looking up from her notepad.

"I think we'll have to do it discreetly. We can maybe make some notes or something," Daniel suggested, reaching into his school bag for his notebook.

"I can write it up with Claire and make some copies. My parents are gone tomorrow, and I can use the copy machine," Beatrice offered, "they won't mind."

"I like that plan," Auryn smiled.

The rest of the time was spent making plans and sharing ideas for the pep rally, which was now only one week away. Auryn felt inspired and even offered to speak at the rally.

HER LOWEST MOMENT

The rest of the week went by pretty smoothly. Beatrice's usual outbursts to a now almost permanent crowd came to be expected. The whole school felt like it was buzzing with excitement, everything felt like it was in its place.

Auryn felt her heart skip a beat when it was time for the pep rally. Excitement filled her entire body while she followed the crowd into the gymnasium. This was the day her friends had been planning for a while now. She couldn't believe it was here!

She could feel the connection she and her friends had, exchanging high fives and laughing as they found their bench. It had only been a short time, but she felt the common desire they all had to break free.

"Where are Beatrice and Claire?" Auryn asked, turning to Daniel.

"The teachers asked them up. They'll be making some announcements soon," he whispered.

A quick tap to the mic drew everyone's attention. The principal stood there preparing to speak to the now silent gym.

"Thank you for gathering with us today. It's been

an honor to see the effort everyone has put in this year," he smiled, straightening his notes, "as a celebration, we're going to have a few of our students announce their surprise!"

Auryn's heart raced a million miles a minute, she was the one Beatrice had wanted to announce their plan. Her legs shook as she stood up and made her way to the podium next to where he was standing. She took a deep breath and grabbed the mic. Everyone was relying on her to get the ball rolling. Her eyes found her parents in the crowd.

"Hello everyone! I'm Auryn! I'm here to share a message with you guys today. My new friends and I are here to deliver it! So, it's my pleasure to announce your class president candidate Beatrice. She's gonna tell you all about our idea. Give it up for her!"

The audience cheered respectfully as Beatrice skipped out, Claire following close behind. Auryn caught Emma writing things down and smiled to herself. Beatrice seemed to be freezing up as she took the microphone from Auryn. Noticing this, Auryn placed her hand on Bea's shoulder, "you've got this!"

With a quick smile, Beatrice raised the mic. While she spoke, Auryn scanned the crowd of parents, they seemed to be a mixed bag of emotions.

"Hello, I'm Bea! I'm here today to ask for love and encouragement from the adults in our audience on behalf of the kids here. We want to share with you our hopes and desires for the future. We want to be free to express ourselves and appreciate what makes us unique, but also what makes us similar. As the president, I will make a difference…"

After speaking, Beatrice signaled to the kids behind her, who joined hands. The crowd was restless, but the kids on stage didn't seem to notice, they could only feel each other. Daniel was the first to step up, in his pink shirt again, he took the mic.

"I'm Daniel, and…" he took a deep breath, "I'm gay. But there's more to me than that. I'm afraid of what people will think of me. But I want to be free to do what I do. I love writing and stories and I want to move to New York! I'm strong, and I'm brave," his breath hitched in his throat when the audience didn't respond, it was almost as if they were frozen. Auryn took the initiative and clapped, the audience slowly followed suit.

Daniel helped Lena onto the stage next. She didn't hesitate to speak as the crowd died down.

"Hi, I'm Lena. And I…I want to help people. I want to stop the fighting and disrespect. I'm strong, I'm smart, and I can put an end to the hatred between people."

A couple other kids went up after and spoke their truth. Auryn could almost see the fear radiating off them, she felt it was too big a leap for them and she began to panic!

"Let's call if off here," she whispered to Beatrice.

"What? Why? Auryn, what are you talking about?" Beatrice looked confused, and scared.

Auryn could barely control what she was saying,

"Let's call it off! It was just a joke!"

She must have spoken a little too loud, because a gasp from the crowd snapped her head up. It seemed like most of the audience had heard. She felt her stomach drop and looked to her friends for guidance.

The only thing she was met with were faces of hurt and betrayal. She had acted out and lost herself. She betrayed the people who had supported her in that moment. Her head whipped around to face Beatrice, but she started backing away.

Oh no.

"I... I..." Auryn stuttered. The audience began to clatter, she felt the entire room spinning around her.

"Alright, alright everyone, let's hear it for Beatrice!" The principal called.

Auryn could barely hear the crowd.

INTO THE SUN

"May I come in?" her Father spoke.

Auryn was in her bed, eyes facing the wall. It was only Friday, but she couldn't bring herself to go to school. With the blankets piled over her head, she gave a small, "yeah, go ahead."

Auryn had never felt so ashamed in her life. She hurt the people closest to her, her best friends. She tried to fix it and she failed. She shut out her Father, her guiding light. His touch to her shoulder was like a wake-up call.

"I'm here, Auryn."

She raised her head to look at him, as if she were looking in a mirror. His face was painted with a sad smile.

"You're going to be okay."

She certainly didn't feel okay. She choked back tears as she looked at her Father.

"I'm so sorry, Father."

"You were forgiven long ago."

"I'm the one that needs your forgiveness, Auryn," her Mother's voice called to her. She felt like she was speaking to herself in the mirror, which was across from her bed.

"I love you, Mother! I forgive you!" Auryn reached for her Mother but couldn't find her.

Auryn's forgiveness radiated a light which she could feel all around her. Her empathy knew no bounds and she felt for her Mother. The light she was feeling might have been intensified by what was radiating through her window. Stepping into its rays, the window illuminated, she glanced outside her home.

The field outside held the same golden grass, swaying gently in the wind. The rain that had occurred earlier, which only fueled her bad mood, was beginning to go away. Taking its place was a large double rainbow. She turned to show her parents the lovely sight, but they had left the room.

She felt comfort knowing they were always with her, even if not physically. They were giving her time to reconnect with herself. Losing who she was was something Auryn had never experienced before. When she panicked, she forgot who she was, it was foreign and terrifying.

While brief, Auryn felt like she was winning her battle with darkness—with losing herself. Her parents had been the key to that, to helping her embrace who she was. She was lucky, she was raised with the right tools. Some people never get that chance.

"Father?" she poked her head out of her room.

"What is it?" he asked politely.

"I think I'm ready to go back."

"Welcome back then, Auryn."

THE FINAL GATHERING

The school felt overwhelmed with sadness, even as Auryn came in. But she didn't let it get to her. She was going to fix this, but in her own way. This was something she would do—it wasn't like before.

She saw her friends, the five of them, huddled together. Despite everything she had said, despite everything she had done, they held their arms to her and she fell right in.

"What's going on?" she asked, pulling out of the hug. Her tone was authentically curious as she scanned her friends' faces.

"There's hope, Auryn, there's still hope!" Daniel exclaimed.

"Tell me more!" the words almost fell out of her mouth.

She could almost hear her Mother's voice, "You weren't responsible, let it be." She felt like she understood, like she finally aligned with her parents, they were a trinity. It was like she had full access to everything. It was like she could see every side, she just had to be it, live it.

Daniel's final word, "hope," reverberated in her

mind. While Auryn hoped this would work, she needed to face her actions to move forward and she was ready.

"The other kids are really upset," Emma told her, "their parents didn't get the message we wanted them to."

Auryn simply nodded.

"And the other kids, they aren't allowed to talk to us anymore. It's awful!" Lena started to yell but was hushed by Daniel.

"I am so sorry. I should have been here for you, for all of you." Auryn looked at her friends, they hadn't abandoned her, but she had. "I won't let it happen again, I won't do it again."

Beatrice gave her a smile, "What matters is that you're here now, you came back for us. Thank you for apologizing, Auryn, I forgive you."

"I do too," Claire told her.

"And me," Emma spoke up.

"Same here," Daniel added.

The group looked to Lena.

"I-I do too...or whatever," Lena folded her arms and looked away. Auryn could see a small smile tugging at the corners of her lips.

"But, Auryn," Emma spoke up, "the other parents might not have gotten it, but ours did!"

Auryn's jaw dropped, she couldn't believe it. Before she could form words, Beatrice spoke.

"They saw how vibrant and happy we were. But then after the pep rally, they got to see how down we were too. They wanted us to be happy, so they want to help us inspire other parents."

"And Auryn, you won't believe it," Daniel burst out, "my dad was the one who called everyone together—he led the way!"

"That's amazing, we're doing it!" Auryn cheered.

The suffocating sadness that clung to the school was wiping away. The air felt clean. They could breathe easy again. They could understand what they needed to do next.

"My hope," Auryn began, "is that you can all trust yourselves enough to just be you. Leading by example, like I had said—"

"But didn't that not work?" Emma interrupted, "isn't that what got us into this mess?"

"What got us into this mess was forcing others to face themselves. I don't know how I didn't see it sooner, but instead of forcing others, we can just role model. We don't push it in their face, we just exist as *us*. Can we do it?"

The five looked at each other, and then at Auryn. "Yes we can!" they cheered.

"Did I...just do that?" Auryn wondered.

"You did," the voices of her Mother and Father spoke in unison, together at last. She's back!

"We're going to plant the seed," Auryn said aloud, "we'll be free, we can play, we can laugh, it's okay!"

They were headed down the right path and it was big enough for everyone. As they walked into the light, they could hear footsteps behind them.

AND SO IT BEGINS...

"Annie, it's morning, wake up," the Father spoke.

I open my eyes and see the familiar surroundings of my room and my notebook on my nightstand. Today is a big day for me, and I'm ready.

"What do I wear today?" I say aloud, rifling through the clothes in my closet.

This day is already feeling like a dream, even though I just woke up. This day has been coming my whole life. The days of holding myself back are over, all I need to do is show up.

I look in the mirror, look right into my eyes and say to myself, "You have so got this!"

Nothing in the world can make me waver. Self-confidence radiates from me as I step into my shoes and find my bag and my keys.

On my way out, I grab my white jacket and welcome the unknown.

ANNIE CLARK

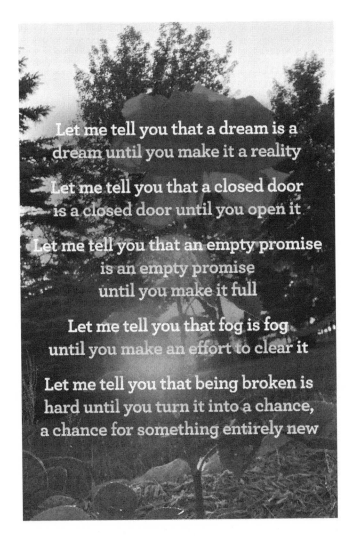

Let me tell you that a dream is a
dream until you make it a reality

Let me tell you that a closed door
is a closed door until you open it

Let me tell you that an empty promise
is an empty promise
until you make it full

Let me tell you that fog is fog
until you make an effort to clear it

Let me tell you that being broken is
hard until you turn it into a chance,
a chance for something entirely new

POETRY & PHOTOGRAPHY
Marie Streadwick 2019

81

ANNIE CLARK

DISCUSSION QUESTIONS

Let's break the spell.

My team and I created these questions to help you get more out of the book; asking questions you might not have pondered on your own. These questions are intended to delve a bit deeper into why living free and authentically may never happen for some. Knowing what I know now drives me to share – *the truth is: living your dream can be a reality!*

Engaging in open discussion about what you read can make the book more meaningful by exploring and sharing your own thoughts and feelings, while hearing and considering others' views; which likely differ from your own. The takeaways may be subtle insights or monumental discoveries which could be the spark that transforms your life.

We encourage you to approach each question with a curious and open mind, and to ponder, reflect, discover, and maybe uncover a point of view you never knew you had.

These questions can be used to launch discussions for youths, adults, families, teachers, counselors, coaches, spiritual and religious leaders – anyone who wants more for themselves, their neighbors, communities, and those they love. Please join us in looking inside ourselves and connecting with others to unite in the name of love and liberation for ourselves and for others.

Please share your thoughts, answers, and/or questions! Email **bravuralifestrategies@gmail.com**.

Here's a tip: Reading the book more than once (3x is optimal) and engaging in exploration and discussion helps you expand. And would you look at that…we purposely gave you, the reader, space to write 'cuz that's what we do – *lucky you, a workbook for free!*

Here we go:

1. Who is Auryn and who/what does she represent?

   _____

   _____

   _____

   _____

   _____

   _____

   _____

2. Who is Auryn's Father and who/what does he represent?

    _____

    _____

    _____

    _____

    _____

    _____

    _____

3. Who is Auryn's Mother and who/what does she represent?

    _____

    _____

    _____

    _____

    _____

    _____

    _____

4. Why do you think Auryn's parents chose to make the move?

_____

_____

_____

_____

_____

_____

_____

5. Where was Auryn raised? Where did she move to? What is the relevance?

_____

_____

_____

_____

_____

_____

_____

6. What does Auryn's notebook symbolize?

    _____

    _____

    _____

    _____

    _____

    _____

    _____

7. Who is on the cover of the book and what is the
    significance of the butterflies in her hair?

    _____

    _____

    _____

    _____

    _____

    _____

    _____

8. Why do you think Auryn so desperately wants to help people? Why do you think she fell into the belief she could save people? If you can relate, why do you think you want to help/save others?

_____

_____

_____

_____

_____

_____

_____

9. What part of Auryn's Mother still resides within her? Why doesn't that part dominate?

_____

_____

_____

_____

_____

_____

_____

10. Why do all the kids relate to each other when they all have a different upbringing and different interests? What do you relate to?

_____

_____

_____

_____

_____

_____

_____

11. What do all the kids have in common? What do the parent/adults have in common? What do they all have in common?

_____

_____

_____

_____

_____

_____

_____

12. Which character do you relate to most and why?

_____

_____

_____

_____

_____

_____

_____

13. Why does Daniel's father have a name when the other parents don't? Why is Daniel's father named Noah?

_____

_____

_____

_____

_____

_____

_____

14. Why are Bea's mother, both of Lena's parents, and Daniel's father important?

_____

_____

_____

_____

_____

_____

_____

15. How is Auryn's Father different from the other fathers in this story? How are they similar?

_____

_____

_____

_____

_____

_____

_____

16. Why do you think the kids fear being themselves in front of their parents?

_____

_____

_____

_____

_____

_____

17. Why does it seem the parents need the kids to stay the way they are? Why do you think change can feel so threatening to parents? Where do you think parents' fear comes from?

_____

_____

_____

_____

_____

_____

_____

18. Do you think parents experience(d) the same thing with their parents?

_____

_____

_____

_____

_____

_____

_____

19. Why is it so important for parents/adults to be in a good place emotionally?

_____

_____

_____

_____

_____

_____

_____

20. How do you think our fear of what our parents think of us plays out for the people in our everyday life? If this is true for you, how is it evident in your own experience, whether you are an adult or young adult?

_____

_____

_____

_____

_____

_____

_____

21. What is the moral of this story?

_____

_____

_____

_____

_____

_____

_____

22. Why do you think the first and the last chapter have the same name: And So It Begins…?

_____

_____

_____

_____

_____

_____

_____

23. What is the significance of the white jacket?

_____

_____

_____

_____

_____

_____

_____

24. Why do you think we struggle to be our true selves?

_____

_____

_____

_____

_____

_____

_____

25. Why do you think we are so focused on what other people think of us?

_____

_____

_____

_____

_____

_____

_____

26. Daniel had been so afraid to wear his pink shirt, why do you think he only received compliments when he finally wore it?

_____

_____

_____

_____

_____

_____

_____

27. How does what others think or say affect your decisions or feelings about yourself?

_____

_____

_____

_____

_____

_____

_____

28. What does your dream look like? What does "living your dream" mean to you?

_____

_____

_____

_____

_____

_____

_____

29. Are you holding yourself back from living your dream? Why? What do you think is in your way?

_____

_____

_____

_____

_____

_____

_____

30. The title includes, 'A Guide to the Key of Life'; what do you think that means? What do you think the 'Key' to life is and how do you think you get it?

_____

_____

_____

_____

_____

_____

_____

31. Can you identify the self-talk in your head when you want to be yourself but can't? What is it saying?

_____

_____

_____

_____

_____

_____

_____

32. Who is the real you? Who has met the real you?

_____

_____

_____

_____

_____

_____

_____

33. Where do you think our self-worth originates?

_____

_____

_____

_____

_____

_____

_____

34. Do new beginnings and change require self-forgiveness? If so, why?

_____

_____

_____

_____

_____

_____

_____

35. "Wherever you go, there you are." Do you think that's true? What does that saying mean to you?

_____

_____

_____

_____

_____

_____

_____

36. If you felt completely free to be who you truly are, without judgement from yourself or others, what would you do/say?

_____

_____

_____

_____

_____

_____

_____

37. If you had the desire, what would be your plan for uncovering/revealing your authentic you?

_____

_____

_____

_____

_____

_____

_____

YOUR NOTES:

Be they little or big, you never know what they might spark...

ACKNOWLEDGMENTS

Thank you to my husband TJ Clark, for keeping life fun! For your generous unconditional soul and continuously, selflessly, loving me as I am – flawed, imperfect, and driven with passion for liberation. The thing I'm most proud of is being your wife.

Thank you to my beloved nieces and nephews for bringing me more joy than one deserves and giving me just one more reason to keep going! And a special thank you to: Claude, for the brilliant words that pour from the depths of your heart and your soul—they will travel the world; Reagan, for your dazzling artwork and creativity that brightens even the stars; Marie, for your stunning photograph and for your poem that flows as beautifully and naturally as your spoken word that echoes in the night.

Thank you to my parents and my family for always believing in my vision and potential and never needing me to be anything more than I am. And to Papa and Mama Clark, Jeff, Christy, Natalie, and Aunt Jill for your unconditional love. You freaking rock—I love being a Clark!

Thank you to Andrea Koch, whom I am blessed to have as my partner in this glorious and fulfilling

business! Your genius, presence, grace, charm, generosity, and unconditional love touch the hearts of everyone lucky enough to know you.

Thank you, Heather, for never having a doubt, and designing everything I envision and giving it life. You blow me away every time!

Thank you, Signe, for stepping in when I need it most for so many years and for your generous input and expertise.

Thank you, Gretchen Overbeek, for jumping in to guide me, for making me laugh, and for helping me not take myself too seriously!

Thank you, Jen Kreta, for your friendship and for your amazing gift to capture the shot!

Thank you, Hollie, for joining the team with your whole heart, without hesitation, and going above and beyond designing our platform for our vision – and then some!!!

Thank you to all my besties! You know who you are...we will grow old in love and laughter looking back on years of sacred friendship.

Thank you to my most cherished clients in the chair – you are my best friends. I'm forever grateful for the years of growth, love, and laughter together that carry me today and will carry me for years to come. Born in the name of hair!

Thank you to Chris Warren and all the talented and generous peeps at Z93 for taking us both (Andrea and myself) under your wing! We are so proud to be a part of such an amazing family!

And I would not be kindhearted if I didn't thank myself, for never giving up on me, and affirming I'm pretty okay just as I am.

ABOUT THE AUTHOR

Annie Clark was born and raised in Traverse City, Michigan.

Armed with a psychology degree and a background studying film and television in New York, Annie moved into the hair industry and quickly became known as a "hairapist." For the last 20 years, she has applied her skills as a trusted friend and advisor to all who sat in her chair.

She is a Life Strategist, Keynote Speaker, the creator and host of the radio talk show Lifelines. She is also Co-Founder, President, CEO and CCO of Bravura Life Strategies LLC, creating the Bravura Method, a revolutionary approach to get unstuck, out of your head, and into your life by helping you discover what's holding you back from getting what you want.

For information on Annie's training and programs please visit **bravuralifestrategies.com** or email **bravuralifestrategies@gmail.com**.

PRAISE FOR THE BRAVURA METHOD

"For me, this class has been life-changing. I'm all about personal development and pursuing the best I can be, so I've read books and listened to a lot of famous speakers, practiced methods, and have comfort in my spiritual life. I expected to have a somewhat positive experience…but I never expected to say, "life-changing!"
– JK

"I strongly recommend this class for everybody even if you feel your life is great. Annie and Andrea have really shown me how to dig deep and not be afraid to express my thoughts. Love to the both of you!! Looking forward to taking class two!" – LD

"It gave me the tools to take action and get past the 'I have an idea stage.' It's the connection of putting together the Why + the How + Do." – CG

"It taught me to love myself and to believe in me." – PH

"One word that describes it: Liberating!" – RL

"It's helping me have the confidence to be my authentic self. It makes me feel supported to grow into a better version of myself."
– BR

"The concept is nothing short of brilliance." – JG

"Everyone can benefit from this class. You'll be able to handle situations as they arise. You'll have another tool in your toolbox. I couldn't recommend enough. The change is immeasurable. This practice will make others ask you, what's changed?" – EN

PRAISE FOR LIFELINES

"I listened to your show yesterday. I feel I need to say, your kindness and your ability to see and hear people is palpable. Not even an ounce of judgement. Just love and acceptance. You are a beautiful human and I love you!" – LB

"I can't believe that sweet little girl that was my neighbor has a radio show! So proud of you!" – TO

"I always look forward to my Thursday night drive home. Thank you for promoting positive self-love and healing." – LM

"I absolutely love listening to you!" – JD

"Great show!!!! Love you! Using the tools with great success!" – JK

"Yes, great job Annie Clark! It takes courage to do what you are doing and I know you are helping people." – SC

"Annie...we're all looking up to you (class of 85) we're backing you up girl. Like I said, that's why we voted you for class president! You got it going on and were all watching and got your back! CLASS OF 85 ROCKS! Love you Annie!" – DS

"This is your mission of love...your mission to guide others!!!! You are doing amazing work Annie Clark!!!! You and your team rock!!!" – DL

For information on Annie's training and programs please visit
bravuralifestrategies.com or email
bravuralifestrategies@gmail.com.

ANNIE CLARK